THE CASE OF
THORN MANSION™

A novelization by Nina Alexander

DUALSTAR PUBLICATIONS   PARACHUTE PRESS

SCHOLASTIC INC.

New York   Toronto   London   Auckland   Sydney

DUALSTAR PUBLICATIONS ™ PARACHUTE PRESS

Dualstar Publications
c/o Thorne and Company
1801 Century Park East
Los Angeles, CA 90067

Parachute Press
156 Fifth Avenue
Suite 325
New York, NY 10010

Published by Scholastic Inc.

With special thanks to Robert Thorne and Harold Weitzberg.

Printed in the U.S.A.
December 1997
ISBN: 0-590-88015-2
A B C D E F G H I J

Ready for Adventure?

It was the best of times. It was the worst of times. Actually it was bedtime when our great-grandmother would read us stories of mystery and suspense. It was then that we decided to be detectives.

The story you are about to read is one of the cases from the files of the Olsen and Olsen Mystery Agency. We call it *The Case Of Thorn Mansion.*

Ashley and I were really surprised when we got a call from Mrs. Busybody. She said there was a ghost in Thorn Mansion! Wow! We never had seen a real ghost before.

Mrs. Busybody said she saw strange shimmering lights in Thorn Mansion. She said she heard weird noises there, too. Of course, we didn't ask Mrs. Busybody what she was doing at Thorn Mansion. We already knew the answer to *that* mystery. She's a busybody! She pokes her nose into everyone's business. She's curious about everything!

But we were even more curious. We just had to find out if there really was a ghost. Could we do it?

We weren't worried. Because we always live up to our motto: Will Solve Any Crime By Dinner Time!

Chapter 1

"Trent! Give me that remote!" I yelled. I tried to grab the TV remote control out of my older brother's hand. But Trent quickly lifted it over his head.

"Sorry, Mary-Kate," Trent said with a grin. "I was here first. I get to choose the TV program we watch."

"Come on, Trent," my twin sister, Ashley, pleaded. "You don't get the TV to yourself."

"And *The Ghost Gang* comes on in five minutes," I added. "You know it's one of my favorite shows."

"Too bad!" he said. "I'm in charge until Mom and Dad get home from work. And I want to watch *World of Lizards*." He grinned at us. "Why don't you two go upstairs and solve a mystery or something?"

"There's only one mystery around here right now," I told Trent. "The mystery of why eleven-year-old brothers are such a pain!"

My name is Mary-Kate Olsen. My sister Ashley and I are the Trenchcoat Twins. We're detectives. We solve crimes. We love mysteries!

We're both nine years old. We both have strawberry blond hair and big blue eyes. We look alike. But we don't always act alike.

Ashley likes to think and think about everything. She takes her time and studies all the facts before she makes a move.

I'm just the opposite. I work on hunches. I always want to jump right in!

But there's one thing we always agree on. We hate *World of Lizards*!

"Come on, Trent," Ashley begged. "Let us just watch half of *The Ghost Gang*. You know how good that show is!"

Trent seemed surprised. "You don't even

believe in ghosts," he told her.

"So what?" Ashley replied. "I still like the TV show. It's great!"

"Yeah, remember last week's show?" I asked. "It was all about ghosts in an old haunted castle. The ghosts wore armor and chased people. It was so scary!"

"Boring!" Trent rolled his eyes.

"Forget it, Ashley." I sighed. "He'll never change his mind."

"Let's go upstairs," Ashley said. "I don't even feel like watching TV anymore."

"Me neither."

I followed Ashley up to the attic. That's where we have our detective office. We share a desk and lots of detective supplies. And we each have our own phone. Ashley's is pink and mine is blue.

As soon as we walked in, our phones started ringing. We picked them up at the same time and answered the way we always do.

"Olsen and Olsen Mystery Agency," I began. "Will solve any crime—"

"By dinner time!" Ashley finished.

"Good!" a woman's voice on the other end of the line yelled. "Because I have a super-spooky mystery for you! There are some very strange things going on in the house across the street!"

"Well, Ashley and I—" I started to say. But I didn't get to finish. The woman started talking again.

"Very strange!" she shrieked. "Shimmering lights! Weird noises! Frightening fog! Of course, there's only one explanation!" We heard her take a deep breath.

"Uh, what's that?" Ashley asked.

"It's a ghost, of course!" the woman replied. "I'm sure of it. What else could it be? Why, I know everything there is to know about ghosts. I also know about everyone and everything in this neighborhood. I make it my business to know. And I know there's

8

a ghost. We must do something about it. When can you come? Do you have any questions?"

"Just one," I said. "Who are you?"

The woman laughed. "Pardon me," she said. "You can call me Mrs. Busybody. Everybody does. Though I'm not sure why."

I glanced at Ashley. We both tried not to giggle. We knew why she got that nickname. A busybody is someone who likes to poke their nose into everyone else's business. Someone who has a million questions—and wants all the answers. Mrs. Busybody was just like her nickname!

"We'd be glad to help you," I told Mrs. Busybody. "Where do you live?"

"On Black Widow Lane, in Transylvania Acres," she replied.

"Oh, then you must live in one of the brand-new houses there," Ashley said.

"Yes, I do," she replied. "But the ghost isn't in one of the new houses." She paused.

"It's in Thorn Mansion."

I gulped.

Ashley gasped.

Thorn Mansion!

We had never seen Thorn Mansion. But we had heard all about it. And we didn't like what we had heard. Scary stories. *Very* scary stories.

Ashley covered the phone with her hand. "We can't go to Thorn Mansion," she whispered. "I don't believe in ghosts. But Thorn Mansion is still the spookiest house in California! People say they hear something howling there at night. Horrible, strange howling."

"That's not so scary," I said. "Clue howls at night. Lots of dogs howl."

"Yes, they do." Ashley looked straight at me. "But there is no dog at Thorn Mansion."

I felt a chill run down my spine.

"Hello? Hello?" Mrs. Busybody shouted into the phone. "Are you still there? Are you

10

coming to help me or not?"

"We have to help her," I told Ashley, trying to sound brave. "There's a mystery that needs solving. And Olsen and Olsen are the ones to solve it."

Ashley nodded. "You're right," she said. "Don't worry, Mrs. Busybody," she said into the phone. "The Trenchcoat Twins are on the case."

"We'll be over as soon as we can," I added. "No ghost is going to stop us!"

Chapter 2

We hung up our phones.

"Uh-oh, Mary-Kate," Ashley said. "I just remembered someone who might be able to stop us."

"Who?" I asked.

"Trent!" Ashley exclaimed. "He's in charge, remember? We can only leave the house if he gives us permission."

Ulp!

"You're right," I told Ashley. "He'll never let us go!" I sighed. "I wish we were next door with Lizzie."

Lizzie is our little sister. She's six. Right now she was playing with her best friend, Isabel. They were probably playing detective. Lizzie thinks solving mysteries is great.

Too bad Trent didn't agree.

"Maybe we can sneak out while Trent is watching *World of Lizards*," Ashley suggested.

"Great idea!" I exclaimed.

Ashley and I grabbed our detective supplies. We stuffed everything into our backpacks: magnifying glass, plastic evidence bags for special clues, and our detective notebooks.

"Do ghosts have fingerprints?" I asked.

"I don't know," Ashley replied. "But they might. And Great-grandma Olive says a good detective is always prepared."

Our great-grandma Olive taught us everything we know about being detectives. She told us that a good detective always carries plenty of supplies and a notebook. We always listen to her advice.

We stuffed our fingerprinting kits into our backpacks and tiptoed downstairs.

Trent didn't hear us. He was too busy watching his lizard show.

We crept past the couch toward the front door. "Almost there!" I whispered to Ashley.

I reached for the doorknob—and spotted our dog, Clue. She came running toward us from the kitchen.

"Shh! Quiet, Clue!" Ashley warned.

Clue is a brown and white basset hound. She has big, floppy ears and a wet nose that's perfect for sniffing out clues. She's the silent partner in our mystery agency. But today she wasn't silent at all.

"Arf! Arf!" Clue barked.

Too late!

Trent turned around and saw us.

"Where do you two think you're going?" he asked.

I groaned. Our escape was ruined by our very own dog!

"We've got a case to solve," I said.

"Don't worry, we'll be back soon," Ashley added.

"Forget it," Trent said. "You're not going

anywhere while *I'm* in charge."

The phone rang before I could answer Trent. I picked it up. It was our mom.

"I just remembered something important," Mom said. "I promised to bake cookies for Trent's class trip tomorrow. And we're all out of sugar! Can you ask him to run to the store and buy some?"

"No problem," I said. I turned and asked Trent to go to the store. He frowned.

"I can't," he complained. *"World of Lizards* is on."

Suddenly I had an idea. "Trent's busy, Mom," I said. "But Ashley and I will go if you want."

"That's fine with me," Mom agreed. "I'll see you all in an hour or so."

I grinned at Ashley. She grinned back. I knew we were both thinking the same thing. We could go to Thorn Mansion before we went to the store!

A few minutes later we were on our way.

Clue rode in Ashley's bike basket. Her long ears flapped in the wind. It was a cloudy day. But it was warm. It's almost always warm in California, where we live.

"I wish Trent had let us watch *The Ghost Gang*," Ashley said. "It might have helped us solve this mystery."

I nodded and pedaled faster. "We never had a case like this before."

We rode for about ten minutes. Then I slowed down to check a street sign.

"Here's the entrance to Transylvania Acres," I announced. "And Black Widow Lane is straight ahead."

"Come on, let's go!" Ashley said.

We biked along Black Widow Lane. The houses that lined the street were clean and new and painted in bright, cheerful colors.

"This place isn't spooky at all," I said. "Maybe Thorn Mansion isn't as scary as everyone says."

Ashley took one hand off her bike's handlebars and pointed ahead. "Look!" she said.

At the top of the hill we saw a huge house. It didn't look anything like the nice, cheerful houses all around it. It looked more like a big, scary castle.

It had once been white. Now it was faded and gray.

The windows were covered with cobwebs and grime. A few of them were broken.

No one had mowed the lawn in a long time. Tall weeds grew everywhere.

"That must be it," Ashley said in a shaky voice. "Thorn Mansion! And it looks even spookier than I expected!"

Chapter 3

I took a deep breath. "Of course Thorn Mansion *looks* spooky," I said. "But we still have to investigate. We promised Mrs. Busybody."

"You're right," Ashley replied. "The Trenchcoat Twins never break a promise."

We left our bikes at the end of the driveway. Clue hopped out of the bicycle basket. She ran ahead of us as we climbed the steps that led to the house.

"It looks like nobody's lived here for a long, long time," Ashley whispered.

"Nobody except ghosts," I added.

I looked at Clue. She was sniffing the front door. That made me feel more brave.

"Clue isn't afraid," I said. "And Clue is

smart. She would know if we were in danger."

We stepped onto the porch. "Should we ring the doorbell or just go in?" Ashley asked.

"We'd better ring," I replied. I lifted my hand to press the doorbell.

That's when I heard the strange sound.

"What is that?" I asked.

Ashley listened hard. "It must be one of the weird noises Mrs. Busybody told us about." She reached into her backpack and pulled out her notebook.

I read over her shoulder as she wrote. CLUE: Heard a weird humming noise.

"It sounds more like a whirring than a humming," I told her.

"Okay, I'll write that down, too," Ashley said. She added it to our list.

"Hey, what is Clue doing?" I asked.

Clue was sniffing hard at the front door. It gave a loud creak and swung wide open.

"I guess ghosts don't believe in locking doors," I said. I was just about to step into the hallway, when Ashley cried out.

"Mary-Kate, look! There's the strange shimmering light Mrs. Busybody told us about!"

Ashley pointed to the tall windows beside the front door. A strange golden-yellow light poured through them.

And then a ghostly shape appeared!

Chapter 4

"The ghost! Let's get out of here!" I yelled.

I grabbed Ashley's arm and pulled her down the front steps.

We reached the spot where we left our bikes.

My heart was pounding hard. "Seeing a real ghost was scarier than I thought it would be!" I exclaimed.

"But we didn't *see* a ghost," Ashley told me. "All we saw was a strange light. And some kind of shape at the window."

"A shape that looked like a ghost," I said. "A very scary shape. So, let's go before it gets us!"

I jumped onto my bike and got ready to ride away.

21

"Stop!" a woman shouted, waving her arms in the air. She ran over to us from across the street.

She was short and stout and dressed all in yellow.

On her head she wore a yellow hat covered with yellow velvet leaves.

She peered at us over the top of her yellow eyeglasses.

"I'm Mrs. Busybody," she said. "And you must be the Trenchcoat Twins. I thought you'd never get here!"

"We got here, all right," I said. "And now we're leaving!"

"You can't leave!" Mrs. Busybody declared. "Not until we talk about the ghost."

"Well, you were right," I said. "We saw the shimmering ghost lights."

"Excellent!" Mrs. Busybody clapped her hands in delight. "Did you hear the ghostly noise, too?"

"Was it a sort of humming and whirring

noise?" I asked Mrs. Busybody.

"Exactly!" she exclaimed.

"We heard it," Ashley said.

Mrs. Busybody nodded. "Then you must have seen that ghastly swirling fog, too."

Ashley and I shook our heads. "We didn't see any fog," I said.

"Hmm. That's odd." Mrs. Busybody frowned. "Why, I've seen horrible, swirling fog coming from that house many times. In fact, I thought *all* ghosts were surrounded by spooky, swirling fog."

"I don't know about that," Ashley said. "I've never seen a ghost before. Have you?"

"No, I've never *seen* any ghosts," Mrs. Busybody said. "But I watch movies about ghosts all the time! It drives my cat Pookie crazy. Animals can't stand ghosts, you know."

Ashley and I exchanged a look. "Actually, we didn't know that," I said.

"Really? I thought everyone did." Mrs.

23

Busybody frowned. "Are you sure you're real detectives?"

"Definitely," Ashley told her. "And we'll solve your case, whether or not there's a real ghost."

"What do you mean by that?" Mrs. Busybody asked.

"Ashley doesn't believe there's a ghost in Thorn Mansion," I explained. "She doesn't really believe in ghosts."

"But you saw the shimmering ghost lights! You heard the strange ghost noises! Doesn't that prove there's a ghost?" Mrs. Busybody asked.

"Nope," Ashley answered. "Those are clues. But clues don't prove anything. Not yet."

Ashley opened her detective notebook.

"What are you doing?" Mrs. Busybody asked her.

"Writing down our new clues," Ashley replied. "I may not believe in ghosts, but there is something in Thorn Mansion. And we're going to find out what it is."

Ashley wrote in the notebook. CLUES:

Saw a shimmering, golden light. Also saw a spooky ghost shape.

"Mrs. Busybody says most ghosts come with ghost fog. We haven't seen the fog. But all of these are interesting clues," Ashley said. "Though they don't prove that there's a real ghost here."

"Oh, you don't have to prove that the ghost is real," Mrs. Busybody told us. "I know it is. I'm certain that Thorn Mansion is haunted. In fact, I'm sure it's Old Man Thorn who's doing the haunting. But I want to know *why*."

"Why? Because he's a ghost," I said. "Ghosts haunt houses! They—"

"Oh, no, no, no," Mrs. Busybody interrupted. "Anybody who knows anything about ghosts knows that isn't true. Ghosts need a reason to haunt places."

"They do?" Ashley asked.

"Certainly!" Mrs. Busybody replied. "If Old Man Thorn is haunting his house, he must have a secret he wants to share. It's up to you to find out what it is. Maybe this will help."

Mrs. Busybody pulled a book out of her handbag and showed it to me.

I read the title out loud: "*Getting to Know Your Ghost.*"

Hmmmmm.

"I think ghosts might be real. And I don't mind investigating a ghost," I said. "But I'm not sure I want to get to know one!"

"You might not have any choice," Ashley told me. "Because I just realized something terrible!"

"What is it?" I asked.

"It's Clue!" Ashley replied. "She's still up at Thorn Mansion!"

Chapter 5

"Poor Clue!" I cried. "We've got to save her!"

I dropped my bike.

Mrs. Busybody tucked her ghost book into my backpack. "I guess you're going back to the mansion after all," she said.

I didn't like the idea. Thorn Mansion *was* awfully scary. But we couldn't leave Clue alone with a ghost!

"We have to," I said. "We'll go back, even if we are scared."

"Good for you!" Mrs. Busybody began to cross the street.

"Wait!" Ashley exclaimed. "Where are you going?"

"Home," Mrs. Busybody replied.

"Don't you want to stay here to help us

solve this case?" Ashley asked.

"Not me," Mrs. Busybody said.

"But, don't you want to meet the ghost?" I added.

"No! I said I wanted to know why there's a ghost in that house," Mrs. Busybody explained. "I never said I wanted to *meet* it!"

Mrs. Busybody pointed across the street. "I live in that big yellow house," she told us. "I'll be there all day. Yell when you've figured everything out! I can't wait to hear the secret!"

Mrs. Busybody hurried away.

"I guess I don't really mind saving Clue from a ghost," Ashley said. "It might be easier than trying to talk to Mrs. Busybody!"

I giggled.

Then Ashley and I crept back up the driveway to Thorn Mansion.

We climbed onto the porch.

We didn't see Clue there.

The front door was still open.

We peeked inside.

"Now I see Clue!" Ashley whispered.

Clue was wandering down the long entrance hall. The hall was dimly lit. We saw her stop to sniff at a flowered rug.

I whistled. "Here, Clue. Here, girl!" I called.

Clue ignored me.

"We have to go in after her," I told Ashley. "Ready?"

"As ready as I'll ever be," Ashley replied.

We stepped through the front door into the hall. My heart was pounding—and I thought I heard Ashley's knees knocking together!

"Here, Clue," I called again.

Clue ran to the far end of the hall. She disappeared inside a dark room.

"Clue, come back!" Ashley yelled.

"Oh, no!" I groaned. "We have to go in that dark room!"

"D-d-don't be scared, Mary-Kate," Ashley

whispered. "I'll be with you!"

I took a deep breath. Ashley and I rushed down the hall. We peeked inside the room.

"I've never been inside a real haunted house before," I whispered. "It looks just the way I thought it would—spooky!"

The room was full of dark, old furniture. Cobwebs stretched across every corner and dangled from the ceiling.

Thick clouds of dust hung in the air. Everything in sight was covered with more dust.

"Yikes!" I exclaimed. "Do you hear that? It's the weird humming and whirring noise!"

"It's really not a humming or a whirring," Ashley told me. "It's more of a whizzing."

"Whatever," I said. "Let's just get Clue and get out of here—fast!"

I hurried toward Clue. I bent down and scooped her into my arms. "Time to go home, girl," I said.

"W-w-wait, Mary-Kate!" Ashley's mouth

dropped open. "Look!"

Swirls of gray fog drifted into the room.

"Ghost fog!" I exclaimed. "And that means the g-g-ghost is nearby!"

My heart pounded with fear. "Let's get out of here before the ghost catches us. Run!"

Footsteps sounded right outside the door to the room.

"Too late!" Ashley replied. "I hear the ghost—and it's coming this way!"

Ashley and I hid behind a chair. I held my hand over Clue's muzzle to keep her from barking. I didn't want the ghost to find us.

The footsteps got closer. I peeked out from behind the chair.

I almost screamed out loud.

The ghost was only inches away!

It was tall and dressed all in white.

A huge white hat sat on its head. A thick veil hung down from the hat. It hung all the way down to the ghost's shoulders.

Gulp!

I turned to Ashley. She was as white as a ghost herself.

"Th-th-that *definitely* is a real ghost," Ashley whispered. "So, I guess you were r-r-right about ghosts, Mary-Kate!"

"I w-wish I wasn't right this time," I whispered back.

"Do ghosts usually have a face?" Ashley asked me.

"I don't know," I replied. "But I don't see any face on this ghost."

"Watch out!" Ashley ducked lower. "It's coming!"

I scooted down and held my breath as the ghost crossed the room. It turned away from us. Then it walked through an archway and headed toward the back of the house.

"Now, let's get out of here!" I exclaimed.

Ashley and I raced toward the door. Ashley suddenly stopped.

"I'm stuck! Ick!" she cried. "I stepped in something gross!"

Ashley tried to lift her foot. A string of dark brown, gooey stuff stretched from her shoe to the floor.

"What is that?" I asked.

Ashley wrinkled her nose. "Ghost goo, I guess," she said. "It's disgusting!"

Clue jumped out of my arms. She sniffed at the goo—and started to lick it up!

"Clue! Stop that!" I cried. I grabbed her and dragged her away. She barked and tried to wiggle out of my grasp.

"I can't let you eat that," I told her. "It might make you really sick."

Ashley gave an extra hard tug. Her foot pulled free. She wiped her shoe on the rug to get the sticky stuff off.

"You're right, Mary-Kate," Ashley said. "We don't know what's in this goo."

"Clue really seems to want it, though." I held Clue even tighter. "Let's get out of here," I said.

But before we could move, we heard a loud *thump.*

"Uh-oh. What was that?" I asked.

"I don't know," Ashley replied. We stood still and listened hard. There was another *thump.* Then a loud *clank*!

"It sounds like it's coming from the basement," Ashley said.

"It also sounds just like those ghosts in armor on *The Ghost Gang*," I replied. "Remember? When the ghosts chased those kids? Their ghost armor made thumping and clanking sounds just like that!"

Ashley shook her head. "But we saw our ghost. It isn't wearing armor," she pointed out.

"Maybe there's more than one ghost," I said. "Or maybe our ghost is keeping prisoners down in the basement. Maybe it trapped them with ghost goo. Maybe it wrapped them in chains. And when the prisoners move, the chains make thumping and clanking sounds!"

We heard more thumps and clanks. Louder ones. Footsteps sounded on the basement stairs.

Ashley and I exchanged a look of fear.

"Whatever it is—it's coming! Run!"

We bolted for the front door. Ashley reached for the doorknob and pulled. "It's locked!" she cried. "We can't get out!"

"That's impossible!" I exclaimed. "I know the door was open before."

I set Clue down and tried the front door. It didn't budge.

"The ghost must have locked us in," Ashley said.

More ghost fog drifted into the hall. Footsteps sounded on the basement stairs.

Then a long, tall shadow crept up the wall near the stairs.

"Oh, no!" Ashley turned pale. "Here comes the ghost!"

Chapter 7

"Hide again!" I whispered.

We raced into the closest room. I shut the door behind us. I pressed my ear against the worn old wood and listened hard.

"The ghost is walking the other way," I whispered to Ashley.

"Good," she whispered back.

I breathed a sigh of relief. Then I took a look around the room. It was shadowy, so I pulled open the curtains. Now I could see that there were shelves everywhere!

The shelves even stood in front of the tall windows.

Some of the shelves were filled with jars of brown stuff. The jars had labels with dates written on them.

The rest of the shelves were filled with books. More books were stacked on a big wooden table in the middle of the room. Even more were piled on the floor.

"Old Man Thorn really liked to read," I said. I picked up a large, dusty book. There was a picture of an insect on the cover. It looked like a wasp. I picked up another book. Inside were pictures of more wasps, and hornets, bees, and yellow jackets.

"He really liked to read about bugs," I said.

"Speaking of reading, can I see that book Mrs. Busybody gave you?" Ashley asked.

"Sure." I handed it over.

She flipped through it. "I thought so!" she declared. "Here's a whole chapter on ghost noises. It says ghosts like to thump and clank around to scare people."

"I guess it works," I said. "I'm glad we can't hear that clanking now."

"Is there anything in that book about ghost fog, or ghost goo?" I asked.

"Nothing," she replied. "But here's a chapter about animals and ghosts. It says animals can sense ghosts. And they don't like them."

"That's what Mrs. Busybody told us," Ashley said.

She whipped out her notebook and added that information to our list of clues.

"And we'd better write down our newest clues, too," I added.

Ashley began to write. I peeked over her shoulder.

MORE CLUES: We saw the ghost! It was dressed all in white. We also saw whirling ghost fog and sticky ghost goo. And we heard thumping and clanking noises.

Ashley looked up. "We still need to figure out *why* Old Man Thorn is haunting the mansion."

"Maybe he misses his bug books," I joked.

"I don't think so." Ashley shook her head. "Too bad we can't just walk up to his ghost and ask why he's here."

"Wait a minute," I said. "Who says we can't? He's right here. And we're locked in the house. We can't get out. So let's just talk to him!"

Ashley thought about it. "Okay. It might help solve this mystery."

We brought Clue along and searched the entire house. We couldn't find the ghost anywhere!

We hurried back to the library to think.

"What should we do next?" I asked.

"I'm not sure," Ashley said. She looked up at the window and gasped.

I turned to see what she was looking at. I gasped, too.

A horrible face was pressed against the window glass!

We're Mary-Kate and Ashley—the Trenchcoat Twins.
We were in our attic when we got a call for help.

It was Mrs. Busybody. She said a ghost was living in
an old abandoned house called Thorn Mansion.
And she asked us to check it out. Wow! A real
haunted house!

We jumped on our bikes. We were on the case.

The old house was really creepy. We tiptoed up to the front door.

And we saw something move in the window! Whoa!
The house really was haunted! Ashley and I raced
down the steps as fast as we could.

Then I realized something terrible.
"Ashley! We left Clue behind!" I cried.
Oh, no! We had to go back to the house
and save our dog Clue!

But Clue had gone *into* the haunted house! Gulp! We snuck in after her. We had to be very, very quiet.

Inside the house it was dark and creepy. I heard a strange whirring, whizzing sound. "Listen!" I told Ashley.

We saw gray fog drifting into the room!
Ulp! What could it be? Ghost fog?

We heard footsteps come from the next room! Oh,
no! Someone was coming! Ashley and I hid.

Then we saw it—the ghost of Thorn Mansion! It was huge and white and spooky! We couldn't believe our eyes!

Phew! The ghost thudded away—and we raced to the door. But Ashley stepped in something gross. What *was* that sticky mess? Ghost goo?

We heard footsteps again! Yikes! We had to hide—fast! We slipped into a small room. It was full of old books about bugs. Hmmm.

There were also lots of jars full of brown stuff. The jars had different dates on their labels. What did they mean?

What did the goo in the jars have to do with the bug books? And the whirring sound? And the *ghost*? We figured it out. Can you?

Chapter 8

"Mrs. Busybody!" I cried. "You almost scared us to death!"

"We thought you were the ghost," Ashley explained.

"Don't be silly," Mrs. Busybody said. "I don't look like a ghost!"

She pushed on the window and opened it wide.

"Ghosts don't wander around the yard in plain daylight," she went on. "The ghost *can't* be out here."

"Are you sure about that?" I asked.

"Positive." Mrs. Busybody smiled. "How's your investigation going? Did you uncover any good clues?"

"Sort of," I said. "Come in and we'll tell

you all about them."

"Oh, I can't climb in and out of windows," Mrs. Busybody replied.

I looked at Ashley in surprise. "Oh, no!" I said. "We thought we were locked in the house. But we could have just climbed out the window."

Ashley groaned. "Do I feel dumb! It didn't matter that the front door was locked! Why didn't we think of that before?"

"I guess we were too scared," I replied.

"I guess a good detective should never get scared," Ashley added. "You can't do your best thinking when you're scared."

"I'll remember that—*after* we solve this case," I said.

Ashley climbed out of the window.

I handed Clue over to her.

Then I climbed out through the window, too.

We were in a small area in the front yard. It was filled with tall weeds.

Mrs. Busybody bent down to pet Clue. "What a brave dog," she said. "My Pookie won't go anywhere near this house. Not when there are ghosts around."

"Clue *is* brave," I said. "That's because she's a detective. She's used to being around all sorts of scary places and things."

"That's true," Ashley agreed. "And it's probably why being near the ghost didn't scare her."

"I suppose it's possible," Mrs. Busybody said. "But it's highly unusual."

"Clue is an unusual dog," I told her.

"Woof!" Clue barked. She sniffed at the tall weeds. "Woof!" she barked again.

"Clue may be unusual—but she's also noisy," Mrs. Busybody complained. "I can't stand a noisy animal. I like quiet, well-behaved pets, like my darling Pookie."

"Clue only barks for a reason," Ashley said.

Mrs. Busybody sniffed in disbelief. "Oh, really? What reason does she have now?"

"Well…she…" I began. Actually, I didn't know why Clue was barking.

"I know why she's barking. She found another clue!" Ashley exclaimed. "Come here and look at this!"

Ashley pointed at the tall weeds under the window. "See? These weeds are all trampled down. That proves that somebody was walking here."

"Of course—*we* were!" Mrs. Busybody looked disgusted. "I walked up to the window. And you girls stomped on the weeds when you climbed out."

Ashley followed the path of the trampled weeds to a muddy place on the lawn. She grinned.

"We may have stomped down the weeds under the window," she began. "But we didn't stomp on *these* weeds!" she finished. And look at what's in the mud!"

Mrs. Busybody and I followed the path

until we were standing next to Ashley.

"What is it?" I asked. "What did you find?"

"Ghost prints!" Ashley stooped down. "The ghost left its footprints in this mud."

Mrs. Busybody took a closer look. She shuddered. "The ghost certainly has enormous feet," she said.

"Or else it's wearing enormous boots," Ashley pointed out.

"Real ghosts don't wear boots, do they?" I asked.

Ashley shrugged. "How would I know?" she said. "This is the first real ghost I've ever met—remember?"

"Let's follow this trail of ghostprints," I said.

Ashley, Mrs. Busybody, and Clue followed me around the corner of the house.

The ghost had definitely stopped at the front door.

"I told you," Ashley said. "This proves that the ghost locked the front door."

Mrs. Busybody looked really scared. "The ghost really was walking around outside? I didn't think it was possible! Oh, my—none of us is safe out here!"

Mrs. Busybody ran back around the house. She raced to an open window.

"Quick!" she told us. "Hide in here!" She scrambled through the window and dropped down inside the house.

Ashley, Clue, and I climbed in after her. We were in the kitchen.

"I thought you couldn't climb in and out of windows," Ashley said to Mrs. Busybody.

"I can't—unless a ghost is after me," Mrs. Busybody replied.

"Shhh! Listen!" Ashley exclaimed.

"What?" I asked. "I don't hear anything."

"Exactly," Ashley said, pulling out her detective notebook. "The humming-whirring-whizzing noises are quieter now that we're inside."

"What does that mean?" I wondered.

"I don't know yet. But I'm writing it down," Ashley said. "A good detective pays attention to details."

Ashley added that fact to our list of clues.

"I don't know about you," Mrs. Busybody said. "But I feel safer now *inside* the house."

Thump! Clank!

"What was that?" Mrs. Busybody asked.

"More ghost noises," I told her.

Mrs. Busybody turned pale. "Oh my, oh my, oh my," she murmured. "I've never heard those kind of ghost noises before!"

Ashley took a deep breath. "Well, you're about to hear more of them," she said. "Because the ghost is coming right in *here*!"

Swirls of ghost fog drifted into the kitchen from the hallway!

Uh-oh!

Mrs. Busybody stared at the fog. Her mouth hung open, but no sound came out. She looked really scared.

Clue peeked out from under the table.

She lifted her head and barked.

Then she raced out of the kitchen into the hall.

"Clue! Don't chase the ghost!" Ashley exclaimed.

"Wait, Clue!" I yelled. "Come back!"

Chapter 10

"Clue, Stop!" Ashley shouted. "That ghost might be dangerous!"

But Clue didn't stop. She disappeared around the corner of the front hall. Ashley and I chased after her. Clue was gone. The hall was empty—except for a few wisps of ghost fog.

Mrs. Busybody tapped me on the shoulder. She was very pale. "Um, you'll have to excuse me," she said. "If the ghost is in the house, I think I'd better go outside. In fact, I'm going home. Good-bye!" She unlocked the front door. A moment later we saw her race across the street.

"Oh, no!" Ashley groaned. "We could have unlocked the front door. I guess we were too scared to think of it!"

"Forget about the door," I said. "We've got to find Clue before she gets in trouble!"

"Let's check the library," Ashley said.

I reached the library first. I stuck my head in the door—and jumped back, rubbing my eyes.

"What's wrong?" Ashley asked. "What happened?"

"The sun got in my eyes," I said. "I've never seen it so strong!"

"You're right," Ashley said. "It was mostly cloudy today. But now the sun is out again. And it's shining right through those jars on the shelves in front of the windows." Ashley looked thoughtful.

"And the jars are shimmering with golden light," I added. "Just like the shimmering light we saw through the front windows."

Hmmmmmm.

My eyes widened. "Are you thinking what I'm thinking?" I asked.

"I'm thinking about the mysterious shimmering light we saw," Ashley replied. "Maybe the light had nothing to do with ghosts."

"Right," I said. "It was just sunlight shining through these glass jars! It happens whenever the sun peeks out from behind the clouds!"

"That's one mystery solved," Ashley said.

At that moment we heard a bark from somewhere behind the house. "It's Clue!" Ashley cried.

"Come on." I climbed out the library window. Ashley was right behind me. We raced around to the back of the house.

"Eeek! What are those weird things?" I cried.

Six white wooden boxes lined the back of the yard. Each box was about as tall as Ashley and I.

The mysterious humming-whirring-whizzing sound was louder than ever.

"Don't look now," Ashley told me. "But I think these boxes belong to the g-g-ghost!"

The ghost stood tall in the middle of all the boxes.

It was surrounded by clouds of swirling, billowing fog.

The ghost's fingers were dripping with ghost goo.

And Clue was lapping the goo off its thick white fingers!

Chapter 11

Hmmmmmm.

The ghost didn't look so scary out in the daylight.

"Wait a minute," Ashley said. "That ghost doesn't look much like a ghost after all."

"Exactly what I was thinking," I told her.

"Hello! Who are you?" Ashley called to the ghost. "What are you doing to our dog, Clue?"

The ghost didn't answer. It probably couldn't hear Ashley over all the noise.

"I wish that humming would quiet down," I said.

"You know, it's not really a humming," Ashley said. "Or a whirring…"

"Or a whizzing," I added. "It's more of a buzzing—like bees make."

"Of course!" Ashley exclaimed. "Bees *do* make buzzing noises."

"Uh-oh," I said. "I just figured something out! Bees don't just make buzzing noises," I began. "They also make…"

"…honey!" Ashley slapped her hand against her forehead. "Of course! And honey is brown and sticky—just like ghost goo."

"Right. Honey looks dark when the light is dim," I added. "And it looks golden when the light is bright."

"I bet those jars in the library aren't filled with ghost goo," Ashley said. "They're probably filled with honey!"

"Now I understand the dates on the labels of the jars," I said. "They must be the dates when Old Man Thorn collected the honey."

"And I didn't step in ghost goo. I stepped in a puddle of spilled honey!" Ashley added.

Just then the ghost turned and noticed us.

It reached up—and lifted the white hat and veil off its shoulders!

I stared.

The ghost of Old Man Thorn wasn't old. And it wasn't a man.

It was a pretty young woman!

"Hello," the woman called as she hurried toward us. "Is this your dog?"

Clue was still leaping up, trying to lick honey off the woman's fingers. I saw that she was wearing a pair of thick white gloves.

"Uh, yes—she's our dog, Clue," Ashley said. "I'm Ashley Olsen."

"And I'm Mary-Kate Olsen," I added. "But who are you?"

Chapter 12

The woman took off one white glove to shake our hands. "I'm Natasha Thorn," she said.

"Did you say Thorn?" Ashley asked. "As in Old Man Thorn?"

"That's right," Natasha replied. "Old Man Thorn was my grandfather. He left this house to me when he died."

"Do you live here?" I asked.

"It doesn't look like anyone lives here," Ashley added.

Natasha laughed. "I know. I haven't been able to come around very much," she said. "Just enough to take care of Grandfather's bees."

"You're a beekeeper!" I exclaimed. "Is that

why you're wearing that strange outfit?"

"Exactly," Natasha said. "This suit is made from a cloth especially woven to keep bees from stinging."

"Then you were never a ghost," Ashley declared. "That's another mystery solved."

"Mystery?" Natasha looked puzzled. "What do you mean?"

"Ashley and I are detectives," I explained.

"We're the Trenchcoat Twins," Ashley went on. "One of your neighbors called us in to investigate."

"She thought Thorn Mansion was haunted," I added.

"Let me guess," Natasha said with a smile. "It was Mrs. Busybody, right?"

"Right!" I nodded. "And will she be surprised when we tell her the truth."

"I'm sorry that we were hiding in your house," Ashley told Natasha.

"Not really hiding. Investigating," I said.

Natasha chuckled. "That's okay. You must

be very good at hiding. I never knew any-body was here. Not until Clue found me. Or, should I say, she found my honey."

"Clue really loves honey," I said.

Ashley nodded. "But there's still one more clue to explain," she said. "What about the ghost fog that follows you everywhere?"

"Ghost fog?" Natasha laughed. "Oh, you mean the smoke! I can explain that," she said.

Natasha held up a long silver tube. "This is a smoke gun," she explained. She showed us how the gun pumped out clouds of smoke.

"Why do you need a smoke gun?" Ashley asked.

"Beekeepers use smoke to keep the bees calm. It stops them from stinging," Natasha told us. "Sometimes the bees follow me inside the house. So I always keep smoke around me there, too."

Ashley flipped open her notebook. She

wrote down everything we had just learned.

I looked over her shoulder at our list of clues.

"Oh, no!" I exclaimed. "I hate to tell you this, Natasha. But there's still one more clue we haven't explained."

Chapter 13

"You may have a ghost in your basement!"

"What?" Natasha looked alarmed.

"She's right," Ashley said. "We heard mysterious thumping and clanking noises inside your house—right before we found out that the front door was locked."

"I locked the front door," Natasha told us. "I try to keep it locked when I'm going to be working back here near the hives. The bees make so much noise, I could never hear if anyone was knocking at the front door."

"Okay," I said. "But that still doesn't explain the mysterious thumping and clanking ghost noises."

"The same noises that ghosts wearing armor make," Ashley added.

Natasha started to laugh. "That may be true," she said. "But there are other things that can make those kind of noises."

"Hmm. I guess you're right," Ashley said. "Sometimes our car makes thumping, clanking sounds."

Natasha chuckled. "And sometimes, so do old washing machines."

I groaned. "You mean, those noises we heard were really from a washing machine?"

"Yup." Natasha grinned. "I was doing my laundry in the basement. But the machine was acting up. That's why I kept going inside so much today, to check the machine."

Oooops!

I felt my cheeks flush red. I was embarrassed. "I guess we forgot the rules of being good detectives," I said. "We forgot to keep an open mind..." I began.

"And never jump to conclusions," Ashley finished. "We were so sure that a ghost was making those noises that we never bothered to investigate them. We'll try not to do that again! I'll even make a note of it." She scribbled in her notebook and shut the cover.

"Well, that's another case closed," I said. "And before dinner time."

Ashley stared at me. "Uh-oh," she said. "What time *is* it, anyway?"

Natasha pushed back the sleeve of her white suit and looked at her watch. "A quarter to six," she replied.

"That means we have exactly fifteen minutes to get home," Ashley said.

"That's too bad." Natasha frowned. "I was just going to invite you in for some tea with honey."

"Maybe some other time," I said.

"Of course," Natasha said. "And don't worry. I'll tell Mrs. Busybody you solved her mystery."

"Thanks." I handed her Mrs. Busybody's copy of *Getting to Know Your Ghost*. "Could you also give this back to her? She might need it the next time she thinks she's found a ghost!"

"Sure—but I hope that won't happen again." Natasha took the book. "Before you go, let me give you a present. Clue will love it! A nice fresh jar of Grandfather Thorn's most special honey." She smiled.

"Thanks, Natasha," Ashley and I said.

"Arf!" Clue added.

We followed Natasha back into the library. She gave us the biggest jar of honey there.

"There's a shortcut out of Transylvania Acres," she said. "It will get you home a lot faster. Just take a left at Wolfpack Way, then a right onto Heebie-Jeebie Street."

"Thanks a lot, Natasha," Ashley said.

I nodded. "And thanks again for the special honey!"

Ashley lifted Clue into her basket. I put the honey in mine. Then we wheeled our bikes down the driveway and rode off.

Natasha waved good-bye.

"Well, the case of Thorn Mansion is over," Ashley said. "And we still haven't met a real ghost."

We looked at each other.

"Good!" we both exclaimed.

"I can say one other nice thing about this case," I said.

"What's that?" Ashley asked.

"It was the sweetest mystery we ever solved." I grinned.

Ashley frowned. "Oh, no!" She groaned. "That reminds me—we forgot all about the sugar!"

Chapter 14

"You're right! There's no time left to stop at the store," I said. "Mom will be furious!"

"So will Trent," Ashley said. "Mom can't bake cookies without sugar. He'll have nothing to bring on his class trip tomorrow."

I sighed. "We'll just have to tell Mom the truth. Maybe she can go to the store *after* dinner."

"Maybe," Ashley said. "But she's not going to like it."

We rode as fast as we could. We made it home just before six o'clock. Ashley grabbed Clue and I grabbed the honey. We rushed into the house.

"Hi, girls," Mom called as we hurried into the kitchen. "You're right on time!"

I took a deep breath. "Yes, but I'm afraid we have something to tell you…"

Mom didn't let me finish. She pointed at the jar I was holding. "Wow! That looks like a great big jar of fresh honey," she said.

"That's what it is, all right," I began. "But…we…"

Mom interrupted again. "What a wonderful surprise!" She beamed at us. "I wish I'd thought of it myself."

"Thought of what?" Trent asked. He came into the kitchen and stared at the jar. "What's that gooey stuff?"

"It's fresh honey," Mom replied. "Mary-Kate and Ashley just brought it home."

"I thought they were supposed to get sugar," Trent said.

"This is even better," Mom said. "Fresh honey will give your cookies a very special taste."

"It will?" Ashley asked. "I mean—of course it will!"

"How much honey will you need for the cookies?" I asked Mom.

"Oh, one or two cups," she replied.

"Great! That leaves more than enough!" I opened the jar and began to pour honey into a small bowl.

"More than enough for what?" Mom asked.

"More than enough to give Clue a special treat," I replied.

I set the bowl down in front of Clue. She quickly lapped up all the honey.

"Why does Clue get a special treat?" Trent asked.

"Because she earned it." I grinned at Ashley. "She just helped us out of another really sticky situation!"

Hi — from both of us!

Sssshhhh! We have a secret. But we'd like to share it with you!

The Trenchcoat Twins love to solve mysteries—but that's no secret! The real secret is that we have brand-new mysteries for you to read! Mysteries that no one has ever seen or heard before!

Our very first new mystery took us back-stage at the famous New York City Ballet. It really kept us on our toes! And guess what? You can have a special sneak peek at this exciting mystery—The *New* Adventures of Mary-Kate & Ashley: The Case Of The Ballet Bandit. Just turn the page!

See you next time!

Love
Mary-Kate and Ashley

A sneak peek at our next mystery…

The Case Of The
BALLET BANDIT

"I'm not sure I can rehearse," Vanessa said. "I'm not sure I can dance at all!"

"Sure, you can," Todd said. "You just have to believe in yourself."

"Maybe you're right," Vanessa said. She walked back onstage and struck her opening pose.

A moment later, Richard rushed onstage. He leaped toward Vanessa. I held my breath as he raised his arms to get ready for their lift.

Vanessa hesitated. Then she leaped. Her feet seemed to tangle together. She tripped and Richard reached out to catch her.

"No! I can't do it!" Vanessa exclaimed. "I'm afraid I'll fall again!"

Todd sighed. He motioned to a young

black-haired woman waiting nearby. She wore a sweatshirt and leg-warmers over pink tights. Her hair was pulled back into a bun. She wore pink ballet slippers on her feet.

"Margo!" he called. "Come here!"

Margo hurried up to Todd. "Vanessa is really upset," Todd told her. "Can you take her place?"

"Of course," Margo said.

Ashley looked stricken. "I don't understand!"

"This is Margo Anderson," Todd introduced the young woman to us. "It's her job to know the role of Princess Aurora as well as Vanessa does." Todd looked grim. "If Vanessa is afraid to dance, then Margo will have to go on instead."

Ashley grabbed my hand. "Mary-Kate, this is awful! Dancing the lead role tonight means everything to Vanessa! We have to help her."

"You're right," I said. "And that means we have to find the missing tiara. But how?"

Hey, Mary-Kate! What's New?

Our New Book Series!

The New Adventures of MARY-KATE & ASHLEY™

Coming in February 1998 to bookstores everywhere

New Trenchcoat Twins™ adventures no one has ever read or seen before — with special collector snapshots in every book! Now you can solve even bigger mysteries with Mary-Kate & Ashley and their dog, Clue!

■▲ SCHOLASTIC

DUALSTAR PUBLICATIONS   PARACHUTE PRE

The party can't start without you...

The Adventures of MARY-KATE & ASHLEY™

"MEET YOUR FAVORITE STARS" SWEEPSTAKES

Win a trip to meet Mary-Kate & Ashley Olsen on the set of their next production!

Complete this entry form and send to:
The Adventures of Mary-Kate & Ashley™
"Meet Your Favorite Stars" Sweepstakes
c/o Scholastic Trade Marketing Dept.
P.O. Box 7500
Jefferson City, MO 65102-7500

MARY-KATE & ASHLEY "MEET YOUR FAVORITE STARS" SWEEPSTAKES

(please print)

Name_____

Address_____ State_____ Zip_____

City_____

Phone Number (_____) _____

Age_____

PARACHUTE

DUALSTAR
PUBLICATIONS

The Adventures of
Mary-Kate & Ashley™
"Meet Your Favorite Stars"
Sweepstakes

OFFICIAL RULES:

1. No purchase necessary.

2. To enter, complete the official entry form or hand print your name, address, and phone number along with the words "The Adventures of Mary-Kate & Ashley™ "Meet Your Favorite Stars" Sweepstakes" on a 3 x 5 card and mail to: The Adventures of Mary-Kate & Ashley™ "Meet Your Favorite Stars" Sweepstakes, c/o Scholastic Trade Marketing Dept., P.O. Box 7500, Jefferson City, MO 65102-7500, postmarked no later than February 28, 1998. Enter as often as you wish, but each entry must be mailed separately. One entry per envelope. Partially completed, illegible or mechanically reproduced entries will not be accepted. Sponsors are not responsible for lost, late, mutilated, illegible, stolen, postage-due, incomplete or misdirected entries. All entries become the property of Scholastic Inc. and will not be returned.

3. Sweepstakes open to all legal residents of the United States, who are between the ages of five and twelve by February 28, 1998 excluding employees and immediate family members of Scholastic Inc., Parachute Properties, Parachute Press and Parachute Publishing, L.L.C. and its respective subsidiaries and affiliates, officers, directors, shareholders, employees, agents, attorneys and other representatives (individually and collectively, "Parachute"), Warner Vision Entertainment, Dualstar Entertainment Group, Inc. and its subsidiaries and affiliates, officers, directors, shareholders, employees, agents, attorneys and other representatives (individually and collectively "Dualstar"), and their respective parent companies, affiliates, subsidiaries, advertising, promotion and fulfillment agencies, and the persons with whom each of the above are domiciled. Offer void where prohibited or restricted.

4. Odds of winning depend on total number of entries received. All prizes will be awarded. Winner will be randomly drawn on or about March 5, 1998 by Scholastic Inc., whose decisions are final. Potential winners will be notified by mail and potential winners and traveling companions will be required to sign and return an affidavit of eligibility. Prizes won by minors will be awarded to parent or legal guardian who must sign and return all required legal documents. By acceptance of their prize, winner and traveling companions consent to the use of their names, photographs, likeness, and personal information by Scholastic Inc., Parachute, Dualstar, and for publicity purposes without further compensation except where prohibited.

5. One (1) Grand Prize Winner will receive a trip for four to the set of Mary-Kate & Ashley's next production, located in Los Angeles, California. Trip consists of round-trip coach air transportation for four people from the major airport nearest winner's home to Los Angeles Airport; hotel accommodations for two (2) nights (two rooms or a quad room); and a visit to the set of the production to meet Mary-Kate and Ashley Olsen. Accommodations are room and tax only. Winner and traveling companions are responsible for all incidentals and all other charges, except the hotel tax, including but without limitations to meals, gratuities, all taxes and transfers. Dualstar, Parachute, and Scholastic Inc. reserve the right to substitute another prize if winner is unable to utilize prize within the time frame of the production schedule. (Total approximate retail value: $3,700.00)

6. Prize is non-transferable and cannot be sold or redeemed for cash. No cash substitute available. Any federal, state or local taxes are the responsibility of the winner.

7. Additional terms: By participating, entrants agree a) to the official rules and decisions of the judges which will be final in all respects; and b) to release, discharge and hold harmless Scholastic Inc., Parachute, Dualstar, and their affiliates, subsidiaries and advertising and promotion agencies from and against any and all liability or damages associated with acceptance, use or misuse of any prize received in this sweepstakes.

8. To obtain the name of the winner, please send your request and a self-addressed stamped envelope (excluding residents of Vermont and Washington) after March 5, 1998 to The Adventures of Mary-Kate & Ashley™ "Meet Your Favorite Stars" Sweepstakes Winners List, c/o Scholastic Trade Marketing Dept., P.O. Box 7500, Jefferson City, MO 65102-7500.

High-Falootin' Fun for the Whole Family!

OWN IT ON VIDEO!

The Adventures of MARY-KATE & ASHLEY™

Look for the best-selling detective home video episodes.

The Case Of The Volcano Mystery™ **NEW**	53336-3
The Case Of The United States Navy Adventure™ **NEW**	53337-3
The Case Of The Hotel Who•Done•It™	53328-3
The Case Of The Shark Encounter™	53320-3
The Case Of The U.S. Space Camp® Mission™	53321-3
The Case Of The Fun House Mystery™	53306-3
The Case Of The Christmas Caper™	53305-3
The Case Of The Sea World® Adventure™	53301-3
The Case Of The Mystery Cruise™	53302-3
The Case Of The Logical i Ranch™	53303-3
The Case Of Thorn Mansion™	53300-3

YOU'RE INVITED TO MARY-KATE & ASHLEY'S™

Join the fun!

You're Invited To Mary-Kate & Ashley's™ Sleepover Party™	53307-3
You're Invited To Mary-Kate & Ashley's™ Hawaiian Beach Party™	53329-3

And also available:

Mary-Kate and Ashley Olsen: Our First Video™	53304-3

DUALSTAR VIDEO

It doesn't matter if you live around the corner...
or around the world...
If you are a fan of Mary-Kate and Ashley Olsen,
you should be a member of

MARY-KATE + ASHLEY'S FUN CLUB™

Here's what you get:
Our Funzine™
An autographed color photo
Two black & white individual photos
A full size color poster
An official **Fun Club**™ membership card
A **Fun Club**™ school folder
Two special **Fun Club**™ surprises
A holiday card
Fun Club™ collectibles catalog
Plus a **Fun Club**™ box to keep everything in

To join Mary-Kate + Ashley's Fun Club™, fill out the form
below and send it along with

U.S. Residents – $17.00
Canadian Residents – $22 U.S. Funds
International Residents – $27 U.S. Funds

**MARY-KATE + ASHLEY'S FUN CLUB™
859 HOLLYWOOD WAY, SUITE 275
BURBANK, CA 91505**

NAME:_____

ADDRESS:_____

CITY:_____STATE:_____ZIP:_____

PHONE: (____) _____BIRTHDATE:_____